Pet Show Prize

ROSIE BANKS

ORCHARD

This is the Secret Kingdom

Featherly Farm

Contents

The Cosy Cattery

"They are *so* cute!" Ellie Macdonald exclaimed as she and her best friends, Summer Hammond and Jasmine Smith, watched four fluffy kittens playing chase in an outdoor run.

"What's that one doing, Summer?" Jasmine asked curiously, pointing to a black-and-white kitten creeping along the grass, its body low.

"It's stalking that butterfly," Summer explained, as the kitten's eyes followed a yellow butterfly fluttering nearby. "That's how kittens learn to hunt."

"Can we play with them?" asked Ellie.

Summer glanced to where her aunt was washing up some feed bowls. "Auntie Jane, is it OK if we go in with the kittens?"

"Of course," her aunt called. "Just make sure you shut the gate carefully behind you."

Auntie Jane volunteered at The Cosy Cattery – a cat rescue home. Summer had started helping out at the weekends, too. She loved all animals and going to the cattery was her idea of heaven! And today it was even better, as Ellie and Jasmine had come to meet all the cats

Summer had been telling them about.

Summer opened the gate and fastened it behind them. The kittens scampered over. Ellie crouched down to stroke a black kitten who was rubbing against her leg.

"This one reminds me of Rosa!" she said.

Summer smiled. Her pet cat, Rosa, had lovely soft black fur. "Remember when Rosa came to the Secret Kingdom with us," she said, keeping her voice low so her aunt wouldn't hear.

The Secret Kingdom was an amazing

land that only Jasmine, Summer and
Ellie knew about! It was ruled by plump,
jolly King Merry, and full of magical
creatures like elves, unicorns, mermaids
and pixies. The girls had had lots of
incredible adventures there.

"Oh, I hope we go back to the Secret
Kingdom soon," Jasmine said wistfully.

Before her friends could reply, a fluffy
white kitten with black
paws pounced on her
shoelace. Giggling,
Jasmine picked
him up and gave
him a cuddle.
"He's so sweet!"
she cooed. "Why
don't they have a
home?"

"Their owner didn't have room to look after them properly," Summer said. "So she brought them here to find a new family. Auntie Jane says it's much easier to get homes for kittens than for older cats." Summer pointed at a tabby cat sleeping in the sunshine in a nearby enclosure. "Oscar has been at the cattery for six months now. He's nearly ten and not many people want to adopt a cat that old."

The tabby rolled over on his back and stretched out his front legs, letting the sun warm his tummy.

"Still, he's happy here," Summer said. "He always purrs really loudly when I stroke him!" she added with a giggle.

"You're so good with cats – well, all animals," Jasmine told her admiringly.

Ellie nodded. "They always love you."

"Not in the Secret Kingdom," Summer
said, sighing. She looked at a thin, dull
bracelet on her wrist. "All the animals
there are scared of me now."

Jasmine put her arm around her friend.
Queen Malice, King Merry's horrible
sister, had tricked them into wearing
friendship bracelets they thought were

a gift from King Merry. But when they got to the Secret Kingdom, the bracelets turned into horrid black manacles they couldn't take off! Worst of all, the cursed bracelets had taken away their special talents. Ellie had lost her talent for art, Jasmine had stopped being good at music and dancing, and Summer's bracelet had taken away her talent with animals. Their friend Trixibelle, King Merry's royal pixie, had lost her gift for doing magic.

The nasty queen had taken their talents away so they wouldn't be able to stop her horrid plans to take over the Secret Kingdom. Luckily, the girls had already managed to break the curse on Ellie and Jasmine's bracelets.

Jasmine hugged Summer. "Don't

worry. We'll get your talent back."

"Yes, and Trixi's too," promised Ellie.

Summer felt a bit better. She was so lucky to have such good friends!

"Shall we check the Magic Box and see if Trixi has sent us a message?" Ellie asked.

Whenever King Merry needed them to come to the Secret Kingdom, a message appeared in the lid of the Magic Box that the girls looked after.

Summer nodded. "It's in my bag."

The three girls gave the kittens one last stroke then left the enclosure, fastening the gate securely behind them. Making sure her aunt was busy, Summer went to the cattery staffroom, where they'd left their things. When she opened the drawstring on her bag, light spilled out.

"There *is* a message!" she gasped.

"Let's read it!" Ellie said.

The Magic Box had to be kept a secret, so Jasmine quickly shut the staffroom

door. Then Summer took the Magic Box out of her bag. It had beautifully carved wooden sides and a mirrored lid. Words scrolled across the shining surface.

Jasmine read them out:

"Where animals go baa, moo and neigh,
In a farm with fields full of hay.
A magical prize will be presented,
To an elf who makes all creatures contented."

"It sounds like there's going to be another Talent Week award ceremony!" said Ellie eagerly.

"And the award's for someone who works with animals," said Jasmine. "Oh, Summer, this could be your chance to get your talent back!"

The girls exchanged excited looks. It was Talent Week in the Secret Kingdom, an ancient tradition where awards were given to people whose gifts helped make it a lovely place to live. Two of the award winners had already used their awards' magic to break the curse on the bracelets and give Ellie and Jasmine get their talents back. Maybe whoever was getting the next Talent Week award would help Summer, too!

"Let's solve the riddle and get to the Secret Kingdom as quickly as possible," said Jasmine.

As she spoke, a map floated out of the box and opened itself up.

Ellie smiled as she spotted some of the beautiful places they had visited before – the sparkling Snowy Seas where the pingaloos lived, Jewel Cavern full of glowing gems and Lily Pad Lake, where water nymphs rode on giant water snails. The Secret Kingdom had so many wonderful places!

"So, we need to find somewhere that animals baa, moo and neigh," said Summer, her eyes running over the map.

Jasmine's eyes scanned the map too. "Look!" she said. "What about here?"

She was pointing to a little farmhouse surrounded by red barns and grassy paddocks.

"Featherly Farm," said Summer, reading the label out.

"I bet that's where we have to go!" Jasmine said.

Summer hoped so. The little farm looked gorgeous!

"Let's see if we're right," said Ellie.

They put their hands on the jewels on the top of the wooden box. "Featherly Farm!" they all exclaimed together.

Featherly Farm

WHOOSH! A flash of light shot out of the box. It zipped round the staffroom and stopped in front of the girls' noses. With a faint pop it turned into a pretty, blonde-haired pixie on a flying leaf. She was wearing red dungarees and matching spotty wellies.

"Trixi!" the girls cried in delight.

"Hello, girls!" Trixi said. "It's lovely to see you all," she said. "Are you ready for an animal adventure?"

"Definitely!" the girls chorused.

"Good," said Trixi. "Because Pinky Featherly is waiting for us."

"*Featherly...*" echoed Jasmine. "So it must be her farm?"

"That's right." Trixi grinned. "Pinky is the most talented animal trainer in the Secret Kingdom. I can't wait for you to meet her!"

The girls joined hands.

"Oh, it's lovely to use my pixie magic again now that I'm in your world," Trixi sighed.

As King Merry's royal pixie, it was Trixi's job to help the king with her magic. But because of Queen Malice's cursed bracelet, she couldn't do any spells at all – at least not when she was in the Secret Kingdom.

"I had to use King Merry's Secret Spellbook to get here again." Trixi continued. Then she tapped her pixie ring and chanted:

"Pixie magic, work your charm,
Fly us all to Featherly Farm!"

Sparkles flew out of Trixi's pixie ring, surrounding the girls. They were lifted up into the air and twirled away. No time passed in their world when they were in the Secret Kingdom, so Summer knew her aunt wouldn't miss them.

They twirled round and round until the magic set them down on solid ground.

"Oh, wow!" gasped Ellie, looking down at her purple-and-green striped wellies and her dungarees. "Look at our clothes."

Trixi grinned. "Do you like your new outfits, girls?"

"I love mine!" said Jasmine, twirling

around in her hot-pink dungarees and wellies. She put a hand to her head and felt her tiara resting on her dark hair. Her friends had their tiaras, too. They always appeared when the girls arrived in the Secret Kingdom and showed everyone that they were the Very Important Friends of King Merry.

"It's so pretty here," said Summer, who was wearing blue polka-dot dungarees and matching boots. She looked round at fields filled with buttercups and clover. Butterflies and buzzing bees flew from flower to flower and in the distance she could see a little stone farmhouse with roses growing around the front door. There were some barns and small paddocks surrounding it.

"Let's find Pinky," said Trixi, flying her

leaf towards the paddocks.

"I've never seen pink cows before," remarked Summer as they passed some grazing in a field.

"Really?" Trixi said in surprise. "Don't you have strawberry milk in the Other Realm?"

"You mean these cows actually *make* strawberry-flavoured milk?" Summer

said in astonishment.

Trixi nodded. "It's delicious!"

In the next field, sheep with glittery silver fleeces were grazing. There was sweet-sounding music coming from over the hedge.

"Are those sheep…singing?" asked Jasmine, her eyes widening.

"Of course!" Trixi laughed. "Those are la la lambs, they always sing."

A bit further ahead was a pig sty. Big pink pigs with curly tails were wallowing in muddy puddles. Before they got too close, Ellie held her nose. Yuck! Pigs are stinky."

"No they aren't!" Summer objected.

"Especially not Pinky's perfume pigs," said Trixi. "They smell gorgeous."

Curious, Ellie let go of her nose and sniffed. Sweet perfume that smelled like roses and honeysuckle wafted over to her from the pigs. "Mmmm!" breathed Ellie. "That's delicious."

There were even more unusual animals at Featherly Farm. Giant peacocks were strutting about proudly with real jewels glittering at the end of their tail feathers. Fluffy monkeys with brightly coloured fur swung from tree to tree, and chubby brown bears were happily

picking berries from a bush.

"Wow," said Jasmine. "You don't get monkeys and bears on farms in our world."

"Those are magic monkeys and cuddle bears," Trixi explained.

"Cuddle bears?" echoed Jasmine.

"I guess you don't have those either?" Trixi said with a smile. She waved at a tubby brown bear. It waddled over, wrapped its paws around Jasmine's middle and gave her a squeeze.

All of a sudden, Jasmine felt a burst
of pure happiness like a ray of sunshine
flooding her body. She grinned in
delight.

"Mmmmm, that's the best feeling
ever!" Jasmine said.

Summer desperately hoped that the
cuddle bear would give her a hug, but
when she held her arms out, the bear
suddenly shrank back and stumbled.
Summer tried to help it up, but the bear
ran away. Summer swallowed sadly. The
Secret Kingdom animals were scared of
her even when she was trying to help!

"Pinky's so clever," said Trixi. "All the
animals are going to perform wonderful
routines at the Pet Spectacular this
afternoon. As soon as the show's over,

King Merry will give Pinky her Talent
Week award."

"Are those ponies performing too?" said
Jasmine, pointing to a paddock where
three lilac-coloured ponies with dark
purple manes and tails were trotting and
prancing in time to music.

"Yes, they're Pinky's prancing ponies,"
said Trixi. "And there's Pinky!" She
pointed to where a tall elf with pink hair
was stroking a pony. "Come on! Let's go
and say hello!"

As the girls leaned over the white
picket fence to watch the rehearsal, the
ponies got distracted. Two of the ponies
bumped into each other and the third
forgot what he was doing and turned in
the wrong direction.

"Oh dear!" Pinky Featherly said to the

ponies. "You did so well at yesterday's rehearsal. You must try to concentrate and stick to the beat. I know you can do it! I'll show you one more time."

A pink shimmer spread from her hair all down her body and she turned into a pony!

The Show Must Go On

"How did she do that?" gasped Summer.

Trixi giggled. "Didn't I tell you?
Pinky's an Animal Elf!" The girls looked
at her in confusion. "She can change into
any animal she wants," Trixi explained.
"That's why she's so good with animals
– she can transform and talk to them."

"I would love to be able to do that!"
Summer breathed.

Pinky whinnied and then started trotting round, showing the other ponies what to do. Then she stamped a hoof on the ground in time to the music, as the ponies went through the routine again.

"That's it!" Pinky cried, changing back into her elf form and clapping her hands in time to the music. "Well done!"

For their grand finale, the ponies reared up and danced around on their hind legs. As the girls and Trixi applauded, the ponies bent their front legs and gave a deep bow.

"Yay!" cheered Summer loudly. "That was brilliant!"

Pinky patted the ponies and rewarded them with a peppermint each. Then she strode over to the where the girls and Trixi were watching.

"Trixi! How lovely to see you!" Pinky said with a broad smile. Catching sight of the girls' tiaras she said, "And you must be King Merry's Very Important Friends. I'm so pleased to meet you."

Pinky shook hands heartily as the girls told her their names. Her face was tanned from spending so much time outside and her eyes sparkled with warmth.

"This farm is amazing," Summer said. "I wish I lived here."

"Do you like animals, then?" Pinky asked her.

"I love them!" Summer told her.

Ellie grinned. "Summer's animal-mad."

Pinky whistled and the ponies came trotting over. They nuzzled Jasmine and Ellie but shied away from Summer.

Pinky looked at them in surprise. "Go and say hello to Summer," she told them.

But the ponies shook their heads and backed away.

"It's OK," said Summer with a sigh.

"It's because of this," she held out her hand and showed Pinky the bracelet.

"Queen Malice cursed it and now Summer's lost her talent with animals," said Trixi. She explained about Queen Malice's wicked plan.

"How awful!" said Pinky angrily. "Queen Malice must be stopped. If I can, I'll use my award to help you break the curse," she said to Summer.

"Thank you," said Summer gratefully.

An elf with short green hair hurried over to them, carrying a big tabby cat. The cat jumped down and

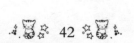

stretched out in the sunshine. It yawned lazily, showing its sharp white teeth. Summer longed to stroke its beautiful stripy fur, but she didn't want to upset it.

"This is Juniper, my assistant," Pinky said. "And Tiggles, the catiger."

The girls introduced themselves and then Juniper said, "While you rehearse with Tiggles, shall I start grooming the other animals for the opening parade?"

"Good idea," Pinky said. "Would you girls like to help Juniper?"

The girls nodded eagerly. As Pinky led Tiggles to a nearby enclosure, the girls helped Juniper as she herded the strawberry cows, the la la lambs, the perfume pigs, the magic monkeys and the cuddle bears into the same paddock as the prancing ponies.

Suddenly, over the sound of moos and neighs, an angry buzzing filled the air.

"What's that noise?" said Ellie.

"Look!" cried Jasmine. A cloud of flying insects was sweeping across the sky towards them. The animals started mooing and braying in alarm.

"It's a swarm of buzzbugs!" exclaimed Juniper.

"Buzzbugs?" said Trixi. "But they usually never leave Thunder Castle."

"Thunder Castle?" Summer echoed. That was where Queen Malice lived with her horrible Storm Sprite servants. She should have known the horrid Queen was behind this!

The buzzbugs were as big as the girls' hands, with whirring legs and hard black bodies. They started to dive-bomb

the ponies,
who reared up
angrily and
waved their
hooves. The pigs
squealed and the monkeys
shrieked as the buzzbugs
swooped down at them.
The strawberry cows swished

their tails and the cuddle bears waved
their paws, trying to shoo the enormous
bugs away. Soon, all the animals were
running around the paddock in a panic.

"They're horrible!" gasped Jasmine,
batting one away from her face.

Trixi squealed
as a large
buzzbug flew at
her and almost
knocked her off
her leaf.

Pinky came
running back
into the paddock.
"Go away!" she
shouted, but the
buzzbugs ignored her.

Suddenly, the girls heard the sound of

hooves. They swung round.

A large black bull was charging straight at them, kicking up a cloud of dust.

"Oh no!" gasped Summer.

The bull had red eyes and sharp pointed horns, but worst of all there was a figure sitting on his back – Queen Malice!

The tall, bony queen cackled as she galloped up to the girls and Pinky. Her frizzy black hair was standing on end and her dark eyes glittered on either side of her pointed nose. The bull skidded to a stop in front of them. Steam puffed from its flared nostrils.

"Tell your horrible buzzbugs go away!" demanded Pinky. "They're upsetting the animals."

"Good!" cackled the queen. "And now

I'm going to upset YOU! You can forget all about getting one of my brother's Talent Week awards!" She pointed her thunderstaff at Pinky. "I can change you into an animal, too!" she said with an evil cackle. "But this time, you won't be able to change back. Let's see how well your animals perform now!"

"You silly elf, you're out of luck!
As an animal you'll be stuck
Unless your creatures are really clever,
You'll stay that way forever and ever!"

There was a bright flash and Pinky vanished into thin air.

"Oh no!" gasped Summer, staring at all the animals running wildly around the paddock. There were so many of them charging about, it was impossible to tell which one had just appeared.

"There will be no show!" screeched Queen Malice. "That pink-haired elf will stay an animal forever and YOU!" – she pointed at Summer with a bony finger – "will never get your talent back."

Shrieking with laughter, she kicked the

bull with her heels. He spun round and galloped away, followed by the swarm of buzzbugs.

"Oh no! What are we going to do?" Trixi said, flying round in anxious circles on her leaf.

Ellie saw that Summer's eyes had filled with tears. She gave her a hug. "Don't worry, we'll stop Queen Malice and turn Pinky back to normal."

"But which one *is* Pinky?" Jasmine said, looking round.

"We don't even know what type of animal Queen Malice changed her into," said Trixi.

"Let's sort the animals into groups," suggested Summer. "That might make it easier to find her."

Now that the buzzbugs had flown

away, the animals had settled down.
They were a bit dusty from all the dirt
that had been kicked up, but most of
them were now calmly munching grass.
Only the brightly coloured monkeys
scampered about playfully.

"Pinky! Pinky!" shouted Jasmine but
none of the animals responded.

"She's got pink hair, so maybe Malice
turned her into a strawberry cow,"
suggested Ellie.

"Pinky?" Summer shouted hopefully, as
they herded the cows.

The strawberry cows looked up from
the grass they were chewing. But then
they lowered their heads again and
carried on grazing.

"Maybe she's a sheep," said Ellie. The
la la lambs were bleating merrily, their

curly silver fleeces shining in the sun.

"Pinky?" called Ellie, rounding up the sheep.

The sheep all looked up. "Laaaaa!" they chorused.

"You can't all be Pinky," said Juniper despairingly.

"Oh, we're not getting anywhere!" Jasmine said in frustration.

"The show is due to start soon." Juniper said anxiously. "Maybe I should cancel it?"

"No, you can't!" said Ellie quickly. "Pinky's Pet Spectacular must go ahead. You heard what Queen Malice said – Pinky will be an animal *unless the creatures are really clever.* I bet that means they have to be clever enough to do the show."

"But the animals can't perform without Pinky's help!" Juniper cried.

"We have to try," said Summer.

Ellie nodded determinedly. "We won't let Queen Malice win."

"No way!" declared Jasmine. "The show *must* go on!

Spiteful Sprites

The girls and Trixi helped Juniper lead the animals to a large barn beside the main farmhouse. It had a sign over its door that read: "Grooming Parlour".

"Pinky thought it would be lovely if all the animals wore purple coats for the opening parade because it's King Merry's favourite colour," Juniper explained, opening the barn door and letting all the animals inside.

Suddenly, there was a flapping noise overhead, and the girls heard some familiar laughs.

"Oh, no!" gasped Summer as she looked up.

Four Storm Sprites – Queen Malice's nasty servants – swooped into the barn, flapping their leathery, bat-like wings. Two of the Storm Sprites threw handfuls of mud and dirt at the animals. The other two Storm Sprites ripped up the pile of purple coats with their long spiky fingers.

"What are you doing, you horrible things?" shouted Jasmine.

The sprites whooped and cackled.

"All the animals' beautiful coats are wrecked!" cried Juniper.

"Ha!" jeered the sprites, throwing mud in all directions.

SPLAT! SPLAT! SPLAT!

The girls ducked and the animals huddled together.

"Get out of here!" Jasmine yelled, chasing after them.

"Yes, go away!" shouted Ellie.

Screaming with laughter, the sprites flew out of the barn.

The girls looked around in dismay.

Now the silver la la lambs had dirt caked
in their glittery wool, and the prancing
ponies' lovely lilac coats were splattered
with brown. The strawberry cows
were so muddy they looked more like
chocolate cows! A little magic monkey
with pink fur sadly wiped mud out of its
eyes and chattered loudly.

"Oh, you poor animals," said Summer.

"Whatever are we going to do?" said
Juniper in dismay. "The coats are ruined
and the animals are all dirty."

"We can't do anything about the
coats," said Summer. "But we can make
the animals clean and beautiful if we
groom them."

"Good idea," said Juniper, opening
a massive cupboard filled with brushes,
combs, rolls and rolls of brightly coloured
ribbons and jars of sparkling powders and
glittery polishes.

"What are we waiting for?" said
Summer. "We can look for Pinky as we
work. Is that you, Pinky?" she asked a
perfume pig. But when she took a step
towards it, the pig squealed anxiously.

Summer bit her lip and tried not to

cry. How could she help find Pinky
if none of the animals would let her
come near them? As Ellie, Jasmine and
Juniper started to groom the animals,
Summer watched them
wishing she could
help. Ellie was
giggling as
the cuddle
bear she was
shampooing
gave her
a hug and
covered her
with soapy
suds!
   Jasmine was
blow-drying the fur
of a little pink monkey,

who kept pulling funny faces and
jumping up and down.

"I wonder where Pinky is," said
Trixi as they worked. "What sort of
animal would Queen Malice have turned
her into?"

"I bet it's something horrible, like a
rat or a spider," said Jasmine, plaiting a
pony's mane. She remembered how the
queen had tried to turn King Merry into
a stink toad before.

"Or maybe something so small we
can't see it easily, like an ant," said
Summer, handing her a velvety purple
ribbon. "I hope we don't step on her!"

The pink monkey scampered on to
the tabletop and chattered excitedly. It
bounced up and down and did several
flips in the air.

"What a show-off," giggled Ellie. "Don't worry, the show is starting soon. You can perform then."

Juniper, Trixi, Jasmine and Ellie worked until all the animals looked sparkly and clean. "Have all the animals been groomed now?" Summer asked as Juniper fluffed up one of the la la lambs' wool.

"Well, all except Tiggles," Juniper said nervously. "But she wasn't in the paddock so she didn't get that dirty."

"Pinky said that Tiggles is a catiger. What's that?" Summer asked curiously. There were so many amazing animals in the Secret Kingdom, but Tiggles looked just like an ordinary tabby cat.

But before Juniper could explain, Trixi called out, "Look! Everyone's arriving!"

Ellie, Jasmine and Summer hurried to the window. They could see King Merry in a golden carriage pulled by two white horses. A procession of elves, brownies and pixies were following him, chattering in excitement. They were all carrying picnic baskets and colourful rugs.

"Should we tell King Merry what's happened to Pinky?" said Summer.

Juniper scratched her head. "I don't think we've got time. We need a new plan for the opening parade."

Trixi nodded. "Besides, if the show goes ahead, Pinky will turn back into an Animal Elf and everything will be fine."

"Quick then!" Jasmine said. "Let's get started!"

"How can we make the parade spectacular without the animals being dressed up?" Juniper wondered aloud.

"I know!" Ellie said. "We can arrange them into the shape of a crown."

"Great idea!" Trixi exclaimed.

The girls tried to help Juniper guide the animals into position, but without Pinky to tell them what to do, it was really difficult. The cows wandered off, the ponies were distracted by the other animals, and the magic monkeys just wouldn't stay still.

"Oh dear," whispered Jasmine. "This doesn't look much like a crown at all!"

"If only we could use my magic to talk to the animals," Trixi said sadly, looking down at her black bracelet.

Summer suddenly had an idea. Maybe she could *use* her bracelet's curse! She strode towards the animals and they backed away from her. If any of them were out of place, Summer moved towards them and the animal quickly stepped back into position. Soon, the animals were arranged into the shape of a perfect crown.

"That's wonderful, Summer," said Juniper, clapping her hands. "Pinky would be so proud."

Turning to the girls, she said, "Pinky and I were going to ride the peacocks in the parade. Maybe you girls would like to do that instead?"

Summer, Jasmine and Ellie looked at each other excitedly. Riding giant peacocks sounded amazing!

Jasmine and Ellie eagerly climbed on to their peacocks' backs, but when Summer tried to get onto hers, it went to peck her.

"It's OK," she said, backing away. "I'll just watch."

Summer suddenly noticed the little pink monkey gazing up at her. "Don't you want to be in the parade?" she asked it, surprised. The monkey shook its head, almost as if it had understood her. Summer grinned. "Don't worry, you can watch with me."

The show was taking place in the

big field behind the farmhouse. Two
elves had set out a golden throne for
King Merry and everyone else settled
themselves on picnic blankets. A brownie
band had set up at one side of the field to
play music for the acts. As Jasmine, Ellie
and Juniper led the animals towards the
field, Trixi flew over to tell King Merry
the show was ready to begin.

King Merry stood up so quickly his
crown wobbled on his curly white hair.
"Welcome to Pinky's Pet Spectacular!"
he announced. "Pinky Featherly has
worked so hard to train these delightful
creatures. Let's give them a warm Secret
Kingdom welcome!"

There was a fanfare of trumpets from
the brownie band and the animals started
trotting into the ring.

Summer bit her lip anxiously. The show was about to begin! But would the animals perform without Pinky?

Amazing Animals

Summer watched from the side of the field as prancing ponies trotted proudly into the ring. The strawberry cows and la la lambs came next, followed by all the other animals decked out in ribbons and bows. The perfume pigs scented the air so that the whole ring smelled of flowers. Ellie and Jasmine came last, riding on the huge peacocks. The jewels in the peacocks' tail feathers glittered in the sunlight. The crowd cheered loudly as Jasmine and Ellie smiled and waved.

King Merry waved back in delight. "Yoo-hoo! Jasmine! Ellie! Hello, my dears!"

"Hi, King Merry!" called Jasmine as the animals stopped and formed the shape of a crown, just as they'd practised. The crowd burst into enthusiastic applause.

When the parade was over, Jasmine and Ellie climbed off their peacocks and joined Summer, watching at the edge. It was time for the prancing ponies to perform, so Juniper led them into the middle of the field.

"I hope the ponies remember everything Pinky taught them," Summer muttered to Jasmine and Ellie. They nodded nervously.

The ponies cantered around in perfect circles, before rearing up and waving their front hooves in the air. They were doing really well until an elf in the audience coughed, and one of the ponies got distracted. It shuffled its hooves in confusion.

"Oh no," whispered Ellie as the other ponies started to go wrong, bumping into each other and turning the wrong way.

"We've got to do something!" cried Summer.

Jasmine remembered how Pinky had marked out the beat by stamping her hoof when she had turned into a pony. Stepping forward, she clapped her hands in time to the music. The ponies nodded their heads, then started prancing again in perfect time. They didn't miss a step for the rest of the routine. When they

finished, the ponies bowed and trotted out of the ring to the sound of loud clapping.

"Phew!" said Juniper as she led the ponies out of the ring. "Thanks for getting them back on track, Jasmine."

Next, the sheep choir arranged itself in a semicircle and began to bleat in perfect harmony. The silver bells around their necks tinkled along with their tuneful singing.

"Wow! They're good," said Jasmine.

The la la lambs left the ring to the sound of thunderous applause.

"The show's going really well," said Summer.

"What's next, Juniper?" Ellie said.

The monkey chattered excitedly.

"That's right," Juniper replied. "It's time for the magic monkey show,"

Four monkeys with pretty pastel-coloured fur ran into the ring. But the little pink money scampered over to Summer and jumped on to her shoulder, playing with her long plaits. Summer

stroked its soft fur absentmindedly. The
little monkey was so playful earlier on,
but now it didn't want to perform.

"Don't worry, I get stage fight too,"
she told him reassuringly.

The other monkeys did all sorts of
magic tricks with their nimble fingers. A
purple monkey conjured
up flowers from thin
air and a light blue
monkey pulled a
fluffy rabbit out
of King Merry's
crown. Ellie even
got involved in the
act, as their assistant
for a trick with big
silver rings.

"Wonderful!" chuckled the jolly king.

Next, the cuddle bears performed an adorable tumbling act, doing roly-polies and even making a pyramid. For their finale, they ran into the audience and gave everyone hugs!

"We just need the last act to go well and that will be it!" Ellie said. "The Pet Spectacular will be over."

"And then Pinky will reappear," said Jasmine. "Oh, I wish we knew which creature she was."

Summer felt her heart speed up with excitement. They were really close to breaking Queen Malice's spell now!

Juniper stepped into the ring. "We will now have a short interval," she announced. "Please help yourself to delicious strawberry milk."

Rushing over to the girls, Juniper

looked worried. "We have a big problem," she told them. "Pinky usually magics up the agility course for Tiggles."

Jasmine glanced over at Trixi, who was hovering on her leaf by King Merry. "Too bad Trixi can't help us."

But the royal pixie wasn't their only friend who could do magic.

"Come on," Summer called to the others.

Hurrying over to the little king, Summer said, "Hello, King Merry! We have a favour to ask you."

"Crowns and coronations!" exclaimed King Merry. "How very exciting!"

"Would you please magic up an agility course for Tiggles' grand finale?" Summer said.

"Why, I'd be delighted to, my dear!"

King Merry said. He scratched his head.
"But where in the kingdom did I put the
Secret Spellbook?"

"Check under your cloak, Your
Majesty," Trixi whispered.

"Ah yes! Here it is," chuckled King
Merry. He pulled the Secret Spellbook
from under his purple cloak.

He and Trixi flicked through the book,
studying the spells.

Trixi suddenly pointed to a page.
"This one looks good!"

"Oh yes! That will do nicely," agreed
King Merry.

"Magic, now make a course appear,
To make everyone clap, gasp and cheer!"

As King Merry finished the spell, a

cloud of purple sparkles shot out of the spellbook. The sparkles whizzed about the ring, gathering in clusters and swirling round and round. The girls caught their breath as they saw a model of the Secret Kingdom start to appear.

"There's Lily Pad Lake!" gasped Jasmine as a beautiful glittering lake formed in the ring with lily pads scattered across it.

"And Jewel Cavern," said Ellie, seeing a shining cave where they had once fought a fire-breathing dragon that

Queen Malice had conjured.

"And that's Wildflower Wood," said
Summer as a copse of trees grew out
of the ground. "And the Enchanted
Palace!"

By the time the sparkles had cleared
there was an amazing agility course
in the shape of the Secret Kingdom.
Everyone clapped as King Merry beamed
with pride.

As the audience enjoyed frothy cups
of strawberry milk, Juniper turned to the
girls. "We'd better get Tiggles," she said.
"I do hope she's going to behave."

They hurried to the enclosure where
Pinky had taken Tiggles to practise. The
girls followed her, with the pink monkey
chasing after them.

The big tabby cat was lying in the sun.

"Hi, Tiggles," Juniper said nervously.

"She's so beautiful," said Summer, admiring the catiger's golden eyes and sleek coat. But she still just looked like an ordinary cat.

Tiggles opened one eye and hissed.

"Sorry about that, catigers can be rather grumpy. You might want to stand back," said Juniper. "Tiggles," she coaxed, "It's time to do your show now."

In a flash, Tiggles sprang up and transformed from a cat into a full-size tiger.

"RRROOOOOAARRRRR!" she roared making all the girls jump back in alarm.

So that's what a catiger is! Summer thought.

Juniper looked worried. "Now, Tiggles, you know Pinky's been training you for your performance today. Everyone wants to see you – especially King Merry. You

have to come and do it," she pleaded.

Tiggles snarled and swiped out with her sharp claws. Then she turned into a cat again, lay down and shut her eyes.

Juniper bit her lip. "Oh dear, she doesn't want to perform."

"But she has to! She has to finish the show or the curse won't be broken," said Jasmine. "We can't give up now."

"But what are we going to do?" said Ellie anxiously.

They all wracked their brains. They *had* to get Tiggles to perform – but how?

"Maybe we could use some treats," said Summer suddenly. "My cat Rosa will do anything for a treat."

The pink monkey ran to a cupboard and began to hop up and down. Summer followed it and opened the door. Inside,

there were lots of cat treats. Taking a
packet out, she handed it to Juniper.

"Here, Tiggles!" the green-haired elf
said, shaking some out into her hand.

Tiggles opened her eyes lazily and
looked at the treats. She seemed to think
about getting up but then decided that
lying in the sun was better than treats.
Rolling over, she stretched, then shut her
eyes again.

Summer's heart sank. "She's not interested in the treats." She rubbed her forehead. This was a disaster. There was just one more act to get through – they couldn't fail now!

Just then, Trixi flew over on her leaf. "Is everything all right?" she asked them, looking concerned. "The interval's nearly over."

"Tiggles doesn't want to perform," explained Jasmine.

"Oh no," said Trixi, her eyes wide. "If she doesn't, Pinky will be stuck as an animal forever!"

"Maybe there's something else we could tempt her with," said Ellie. "What else do cats like, Summer?"

Summer thought quickly. She pictured the kittens back at the Cosy Cattery and remembered how they liked play fighting and chasing butterflies. Of course!

"I've got it!" she gasped. "I've thought of a plan!"

A Daring Display

Summer explained her idea to the others.

"You want Trixi to fly through the agility course to lead Tiggles?" echoed Ellie. She glanced at Trixi who had turned pale.

Summer nodded. "I'm sure Tiggles would chase her. It'll be like when the kitten chased the butterfly at the Cosy Cattery back home."

"But what if Tiggles catches her?" said Jasmine, remembering Tiggles's sharp tiger teeth and claws.

"She won't," Trixi said firmly. "I can fly *very* fast. And if Tiggles gets close to me, I'll just zoom my leaf up out of her reach."

The brownie trumpeters blew a fanfare to announce the end of the interval.

"I'll do it," Trixi said. "We can't let Queen Malice win."

"Are you sure…" said Jasmine.

"I'm sure!" said Trixi determinedly. She swooped around the girls' heads and then hovered in front of Tiggles's nose. "Tiggles! Tiggles! Look at me! Do you want to play chase?"

The catiger opened her eyes. She saw the little pixie and her whole body tensed. She rolled over in one fluid movement, her muscles coiled ready to spring.

"Be careful, Trixi!" gasped Ellie.

Trixi shot away with Tiggles leaping after her. The girls ran out of the barn and watched Trixi fly into the ring. The crowd erupted with applause as Tiggles bounded after her.

Trixi set off through the course with Tiggles right behind her. The first obstacle was Lily Pad Lake. The catiger sprang gracefully from lily pad to lily pad, without a single hair of her sleek fur touch the glittering water. As she leapt off the last lily pad she gave a roar and turned into a tiger. Not stopping to look for Trixi now, she raced up the steep sides of Frosty Mountain, her claws

digging into the snow-covered slopes.
Then she scrambled down the other
side and turned back into a tabby cat
before running towards the trees of
Wildflower Wood.

"Tiggles is doing brilliantly!" said
Summer.

The pink monkey hooted with delight.

"Look at how fast she's going," said
Jasmine as Tiggles weaved in and out of
the tree trunks.

"Go, Tiggles!" cried Ellie as the crowd whooped.

Bounding out of the trees, Tiggles turned into a tiger again and raced towards the model of King Merry's Enchanted Palace. She crouched down and sprang over the turrets before landing and becoming a cat again to crawl through the tunnel-like Jewel Cavern. She bounded out of the cavern and crossed the finish line.

The girls all jumped up and down and cheered.

"Tiggles did it! She finished the agility course!" cried Ellie.

Tiggles changed back into a tiger again, roaring proudly as the crowd clapped wildly.

"Oh, well done, Tiggles!" exclaimed Summer. The little pink monkey jumped onto her shoulder again to get a better view. Summer petted his fur – then suddenly realised what she was doing. Astonished, she glanced down at her wrist and saw that her bracelet was still there. Why wasn't this cheeky monkey scared of her?

"Hello," she whispered, ruffling its fluffy pink fur. To her delight, it didn't try to jump away. As Tiggles finished his routine and turned back into a cat the monkey clapped its paws.

"Well done, Trixi!" cried Jasmine as Trixi zipped back towards them.

"Phew!" exclaimed the little pixie breathlessly. Her blonde hair was a bit messy but she looked very happy. "The plan worked!"

"Good girl," Juniper said, tickling behind the catiger's ears.

Tiggles purred and the little pink monkey jumped down to give her a cuddle. The girls laughed.

"It's so cute," said Jasmine.

"The show's over!" Ellie said to Juniper.

Juniper nodded. "Yes. All the animals have performed."

"That means the spell should be

broken," said Trixi excitedly.

"But where's Pinky?" said Jasmine, looking round, trying to spot the pink-haired Animal Elf.

"Did we miss anything out?" asked Ellie anxiously.

"No," Juniper said, shaking her head.

"All of the animal acts performed."

"Unless…unless the problem is that the show isn't properly over yet," said Jasmine suddenly. "It was supposed to end with Pinky being given her award, wasn't it? And that hasn't happened."

"Of course!" said Summer. "Look at King Merry!"

King Merry had stood up and was looking round, a glittering trophy in his hand.

"But we still don't know where she is," said Trixi in dismay. "What are we going to do?"

"Wait!" said Summer suddenly. "Stay here," she told the others. Taking a deep breath, she walked into the ring with the pink monkey on her shoulders.

"Summer!" she heard Jasmine hiss

behind her. "Where are you going?"

But Summer didn't stop.

The crowd fell silent as she walked across the ring towards King Merry's throne.

Summer could feel everyone looking at her and her cheeks were bright red with embarrassment. The monkey chattered and bounced up and down on her shoulder excitedly.

"Summer?" King Merry said in astonishment, peering over his half moon spectacles. "Have you seen Pinky Featherly anywhere?"

Summer took a deep breath. *Oh, please let me be right,* she thought.

"She's right here," she said taking the monkey off her shoulder. "This is Pinky Featherly!"

The Talent Award

Summer held the monkey out towards the king. "Please can you give this monkey the award, King Merry?"

King Merry gave Summer a kind smile. "Well, Pinky *is* an Animal Elf." Patting the monkey's head, he said, "If that's you, Pinky dear, please turn back into an elf."

Nothing happened. Summer felt her face turning hot with embarrassment as everyone stared at her.

Suddenly she heard footsteps running across the ring. Jasmine and Ellie joined her, one on either side.

"King Merry, Summer's right," said Jasmine.

Ellie nodded. "Queen Malice put a spell on Pinky and turned her into an animal for good."

Everyone gasped. Summer gave her friends a relieved look.

"Queen Malice said Pinky wouldn't turn back into an elf unless the show went ahead," Jasmine explained. "The end of the show is the award ceremony, so she needs to get the award before she can turn back into an elf."

"And you think she's this monkey?" said King Merry.

"Yes." Jasmine sounded less certain. She looked at Summer. "Er, at least, I think so."

"I'm sure it is," Summer said determinedly, stroking the monkey. "She was really helpful and always seemed to understand what I was saying. She kept trying to get our attention. But most of all, she's the only animal that's not scared of me!" She looked at King Merry. "Please give the monkey the award."

King Merry hesitated, then nodded. "Very well, my dears. If you believe this monkey is Pinky, then that's enough for me." With a serious look on his face, the king added, "But a Talent Award can

only be given once. Are you happy
for me to take that risk? After all, this
may be your only chance to get your
talent back."

The monkey chattered excitedly.

Summer looked at it and took a deep
breath. "Yes, I think you should."

"In that case…" King Merry raised the
glittering trophy. "I present this trophy
to Pinky Featherly for all her hard work
caring for and training the animals of the
Secret Kingdom!" He held the award out
to the monkey.

The little creature reached out to
take it. As its pink paws touched the
award there was a bright flash of light.
Suddenly, Pinky was standing there, a
huge smile on her face.

"It worked!" gasped Summer in relief.

Ellie and Jasmine hugged her.

"You were right, Summer!" cried Ellie.

"Oh, well done," said Jasmine.

Pinky held up the award and a bright glow rippled down her from her head to her toes, leaving her sparkling as if

she'd been coated with glitter.

"Thank you for this award, King Merry," said Pinky, beaming. "I shall treasure it forever." She turned to the girls. "And thank you so much for helping the show go ahead, girls. If it hadn't be for you I would be stuck as a monkey forever!"

The crowd cheered and whooped.

"Thanks to Juniper, for all her help, and to Trixi, the bravest pixie in the whole kingdom," said Pinky. Then her eyes met Summer's. "Most of all, my thanks go to you, my dear girl. You trusted your instincts and understood what a little monkey was trying to tell you. Please –" she held out her hand – "I would be honoured to share this magic with you. It is time you got your talent with animals back!"

Pinky touched the trophy to the silver
pawprint charm on Summer's bracelet.
Tingles ran through Summer and she
started to glow, too. There was a loud
crack and suddenly the black friendship
bracelet turned back to the lovely blue it
had been when she first put it on. Queen
Malice's wicked curse was broken!

The audience erupted into cheers again.

Suddenly, all the animals came trotting and bounding and flying into the ring. They surrounded Summer, nuzzling, purring, whinnying, and mooing. Summer hugged and stroked them. It was so wonderful to have the Secret Kingdom animals like her again!

King Merry wiped his eyes with a spotty hanky. "Oh, this is quite splendid!"

But just as the words left his mouth, there was a loud crash of thunder and the sky darkened.

People's laughter turned to screams as Queen Malice suddenly appeared in the middle of the ring. The elves and brownies cowered away from her in fear.

"Sister! What are you doing here?" demanded King Merry. "Go away! You've caused enough trouble."

"And I shall cause more!" hissed the queen. "Much more!" Her glittering eyes

turned to Summer. "So, you managed
to break my spell, did you? Well, there
is still one more cursed bracelet." She
pointed at Trixi. "That pesky pixie will
never get her talent for magic back.
NEVER!"

She shrieked with laughter.

"RRRRRROARRRRR!" Tiggles
suddenly turned back into a tiger and
leapt at the queen, her claws out and her
sharp teeth showing.

Queen Malice gasped in fear as the catiger bounded across the ring towards her. Grabbing her skirts in her hands, she started to run away. Tiggles raced after her, growling. With a terrified shriek, Queen Malice thumped her thunderbolt staff and a thundercloud appeared under her feet. Queen Malice sailed up into the air just in time.

Tiggles growled as the mean queen soared out of reach, then settled down to lick his paws. Everyone cheered again in delight.

Summer glanced at Trixi and saw that the little pixie was looking worried. "Don't listen to Queen Malice, Trixi," she said softly. "We got my talent back and we'll get yours back too."

"We'll do everything we possibly can!" vowed Jasmine.

"Queen Malice won't beat us," promised Ellie.

Trixi took a deep breath. "Thank you, girls. I don't know what we'd do without you!"

King Merry looked at Ellie, Jasmine and Summer. "My dears, it is time for me to send you home. But Trixi will send you a message to bring you back here very soon."

"We really want to come back and help Trixi," Jasmine said, hugging him.

"And so you will," the little king promised. "We will work together to get her magic back."

Trixi kissed each of the girls on their nose and then King Merry opened his spellbook. Sparkles of light shot out of the book and surrounded the girls.

"Goodbye!" Ellie, Summer and Jasmine called out as they felt themselves spinning away.

As the sparkles cleared, they found themselves in the cattery staffroom.

"We're back," said Ellie, blinking.

Summer put the Magic Box away in her bag and then they went back outside.

Oscar was lying on his back in the sun and a friendly-looking lady with glasses and long brown hair was stroking him. "What a handsome old boy," she said to Summer's aunt. "Is he available to adopt?"

Summer grinned. It looked like Oscar had finally found a real home!

As the cheerful lady and Auntie Jane went to fill out some forms, the tabby cat stretched and purred contentedly.

"Animals in the Secret Kingdom might be really different from ours," Summer said as she went to give Oscar a stroke, "but one thing's the same – ALL cats like to sunbathe!" She was so relieved to have her talent back. She'd missed it so much, and she knew Trixi must be missing her magic terribly.

Her eyes met Ellie's and Jasmine's, and her friends knew exactly what she was thinking.

"We're not going to let Queen Malice win," Jasmine whispered.

"Never," vowed Ellie.

"We're going to get Trixi's magic talent back," declared Summer. "No matter what!"

Read on for a sneak peek
of the next Secret Kingdom
adventure,

Twinkle Trophy

Read on for a sneak peek...

A Place of Magical Fun

"I want to try the hoopla," said Ellie Macdonald excitedly. "One of the prizes is an art set!" Ellie and her best friends, Summer Hammond and Jasmine Smith, were at the Honeyvale County Fair. Ellie's parents and her little sister Molly were there too, but they'd let Summer, Jasmine and Ellie go off by themselves to explore the stalls and to look at the farm animals. The girls were having a brilliant time!

"I'd like to win that cute toy lamb," Summer said as she looked at the hoopla prizes. "The real ones over there were so sweet!"

They gave their money to the lady running the stall and took three hoops each. Ellie aimed at the art set, but two of her hoops sailed past it and the third fell short.

"Bad luck," said Jasmine. "I'll see if I can win it for you!" But her hoops missed as well.

"My turn," said Summer. She stared at the toy lamb hopefully, trying to judge the distance, then threw her first hoop. It brushed the lamb's ears, but it

didn't go over the toy. Her second two
hoops missed the lamb, but she did ring
a pack of three fancy chocolates.

"Well done!" Jasmine exclaimed.

Summer shared out the sweets. "Come
on," she said as they munched happily,
"Let's see what else there is to do!"

"What's that over there?" Ellie asked,
spotting a white tent with a colourful
flag fluttering above it.

"It's a magic show," Jasmine said. "I
saw a poster earlier."

"Let's go and watch!" Ellie suggested.

The girls headed for the tent. Lots of
people were already inside. The youngest
children were sitting on the ground
near the stage, while older children and
grown-ups were on chairs behind them.
The girls found three seats at the back.

The magician was wearing a black cloak with a shiny red lining, white gloves and a black top hat.

"Welcome, ladies and gentlemen, boy and girls," he said. "Prepare to be amazed by my magic tricks!" Taking off his hat, he showed everyone that it was empty. Then he put it on a table and tapped it with his magic wand. "Abracadabra," he cried, and pulled out a bunch of fake flowers.

The audience clapped.

"It's fun, but it's not the same as the *real* magic that happens in the Secret Kingdom," whispered Ellie.

Jasmine and Summer nodded in agreement.

The girls shared an amazing secret. They had a magic box that could

take them to a place called the Secret
Kingdom – a beautiful land full of pixies,
elves, unicorns and all kinds of other
amazing creatures.

The box had been made by kind King
Merry, the ruler of the kingdom, because
the magical land was in danger from his
mean sister Queen Malice – and Ellie,
Summer and Jasmine were the only
people who could help!

"This magic show is making me
think about Trixi," whispered Summer.
Trixibelle was their pixie friend, and
King Merry's assistant. She and the girls
had been tricked by Queen Malice into
wearing cursed friendship bracelets that
had stolen their special talents. Luckily it
was Talent Week in the Secret Kingdom,
and once the prizes had been presented,

the winners could use the awards' magic to restore the girls' special gifts.

Ellie's art skills, Jasmine's talent for music and dancing, and Summer's ability to befriend animals had all been returned already. But poor Trixi's talent for magic was still missing, and the girls could hardly wait to go to the Secret Kingdom to help her get it back.

"We have to break Queen Malice's spell before Talent Week is over," said Jasmine in a low voice. "Otherwise Trixi will never be able to use magic again!"

"But we can't go until we get a message from her," Summer whispered. She hoped they'd hear from their pixie friend very soon.

The magician placed a yellow hanky in his hat. When he pulled it out again it had turned red. The audience clapped, but the girls sighed.

Then suddenly, Ellie noticed light coming from Jasmine's bag. "The Magic Box," she whispered excitedly, nudging her friends. Jasmine pulled the bag out from under her chair and they hurried out of the tent and hid behind a nearby tree.

Sure enough, the curved mirror on the top was shining brightly. As they peered at it, words began to appear there...

Read
Twinkle Trophy
to find out what
happens next!

Have you read all the books in Series Six?

Can Summer, Jasmine, Ellie and Trixi defeat Queen Malice and get their talents back before Talent Week is over?

Secret Kingdom

Look out for the next
sweet special!

Secret Kingdom

Candy Cove Pirates

ROSIE BANKS

Out now!

Ellie and Jasmine are having lots of fun paddling in the ocean, but naughty Queen Malice has muddled things up. Can you help the girls by finding the five differences between these two pictures?

Competition!

Would you like to win one of three Secret Kingdom goody bags?

All you have to do is design and create your own
friendship bracelet just like Ellie, Summer and Jasmine's!

Here is how to enter:

✳ Visit www.secretkingdombooks.com
✳ Click on the competition page at the top
✳ Print out the bracelet activity sheet and decorate it
✳ Once you've made your bracelet send your entry into us

The lucky winners will receive an extra special Secret Kingdom
goody bag full of treats and activities.

Please send entries to:
Secret Kingdom Friendship Bracelet Competition
Orchard Books, 338 Euston Road, London, NW1 3BH

Don't forget to add your name and address.

Good luck!

Closing dates:

There are three chances to win
before the closing date on the 30th October 2015

Secret Kingdom

A magical world of
friendship and fun!

Join the Secret Kingdom Club at

www.secretkingdombooks.com

and enjoy games, sneak peeks and lots more!

You'll find great activities, competitions, stories
and games, plus a special newsletter for
Secret Kingdom friends!